A CLOSING CASE OF MURDER FOR EMILY CHERRY

AN EMILY CHERRY COZY MYSTERY
BOOK TEN

DONNA DOYLE

PUREREAD.COM

CONTENTS

DEAR READER, GET READY FOR ANOTHER GREAT COZY...

READY TO SOLVE THE MYSTERY?

Turn the page and let's begin

~

"It's spring, my dear," Emily said with a sigh as she settled down near Sebastian's grave. Her sweet husband had been gone for a few years now, but she still missed him just as much as she always had. The two of them, she'd been sure, were meant to be together. Even though they weren't together anymore, she knew there would never be another man like him. "The flowers are blooming and the leaves are starting to come out on the trees. It's the sort of weather that always used to make you go outside, take a deep breath, and announce that it would soon be time to go on holiday."

They'd had their little adventures here and there. Once they'd gone into London for a big shopping trip, and another time they'd stayed on the coast of Spain. It was never anything extreme. They didn't climb mountains or hike across countries, but there was always time for the two of them to just be together. That was the part that

Emily had always liked best. She didn't have him around anymore, and she thought her adventuring days were over. That hadn't turned out to be completely true, except the adventures were just of a different sort.

"You should see my blog these days," Emily said with a little smile. "Oh, I sure wondered if I was doing the right thing when I started it. Goodness knows I've gone through several different ideas and themes, trying to find the thing that was right for me. I think I have, now that I've been focusing on book and movies reviews. I go down to Alexandria's books regularly to see what's new, and sometimes I'm at the library. Then, of course, I'm at the cinema for nearly every new film. I just try not to have too much soda while I'm there." She laughed a little, knowing that Sebastian would never tell her to cut back on the sweets and treats. He'd always wanted her to have what made her happy, and if it added a bit to her thighs, he never mentioned it.

"That's not to say that I don't still feature some of the pets from Best Friends Furever. I think you'd really like being a volunteer there with me, if you'd had the chance. We always talked about doing some volunteer work when we retired. I have more than enough reasons to get out of the house these days, so I don't really need it as an excuse for that anymore, but those poor animals really need all the love they can get. Rosemary gets a little miffed at me when she can tell that I've been there, but I think she understands." Emily smiled. Her cat had become the most wonderful companion. It wasn't the same as having Sebastian there, of course, but Emily couldn't imagine what she would do if Rosemary weren't waiting to greet her every time she walked in the door, those big golden eyes curious and her whiskers wild.

"If I'm perfectly honest, I think the shelter pets have helped increased the traffic on my blog. Now, that's not why I do it," she added quickly. "Lily said more times than not, whatever dog or cat has recently had a feature on my website is usually adopted within a few days. The only thing it costs me is a little bit of time, and I think that's more than worth it to know those pets are getting good homes." She knew she didn't need to explain who Lily was. Emily liked to think that Sebastian understood that she was the manager of the local shelter in the way that the dead must know about everything. It was a comforting thought.

"I guess what I'm really trying to say is that I've found something to do with all this time on my hands. It's more than making some crafts or volunteering, really. It's sort of a like a whole new career. You know how much I always enjoyed writing, and I thought the blog would be a bit of a lark. Something fun to try. Nathan encouraged me to monetize my site, and I'm actually pulling in a small income from it each month. Money isn't everything, but I'd be a liar if I said it wasn't a bit of a motivator." She'd never really thought she'd make anything off of it when her son had insisted on helping her put ads on her site, and she hadn't even been sure she'd wanted to bother. In the long run, however, it was paying off. Much of that money went back to buying items or food for the animal shelter, which Emily particularly enjoyed doing.

She leaned back a little, enjoying the warm sunshine. "I think you'd be proud of me, really. I did my work just fine at Phoenix Insurance when we were both there. It was a job, but it wasn't really anything more than that. This is different, and it truly makes me happy. I get a nice balance of time at home with Rosemary when I'm writing, but I also get out and see people. I don't think it could be much better than that."

Emily's eyes traced over her late husband's name carved into the headstone, but then they lifted and looked out across the cemetery. It was a beautiful place, though she knew that not everyone would agree with her that a graveyard could be pretty. The sunlight filtered down through the trees, and the new green stood out on everything. Fresh bunches of flowers had been put out on some of the other graves, sending their scent filtering through the air.

But a bit further away, she spotted a tall figure in a long gray coat. He was making his way in her direction, but then he suddenly turned and cut off to the right. Emily frowned. She knew this place like the back of her hand at this point, considering how often she came to visit Sebastian. There were no paths there that dictated the man would have to walk that way. He seemed to know exactly where he was going at first, but that sudden turn made her wonder.

"There are plenty of times when I wish you could talk to me, dear," Emily said quietly. "Sometimes it's just for my own selfish reasons. I also wish you could tell me about that man. I saw him here before. He was standing in front of your grave. I was so touched that someone else had come to visit you besides myself or the children, but I didn't know him. You and I were together for a long time, so it was hard to imagine there would be anyone in your life that I didn't have some awareness of."

She paused as she remembered that day. The man had looked up at her with widened eyes as she'd approached, and he'd claimed that he didn't know Sebastian at all. He just liked to walk through the cemetery, he said, and would stop to visit random graves. But he hadn't stopped to look at any other tombstones, instead heading straight toward his gray sedan. Now he was here again today. It made her wonder of all the notions she'd been storing up in the back of her mind could possibly be right.

"Sebastian, my love, I think I'm going to have to take a break from book and movie reviews, and perhaps even from helping my friends at the shelter. It'll be just for a little bit, but I'm sure everyone will understand. I think there's something else I need to address, you see, something bigger that's been on my mind for a very long time. I'll have to talk to a few people, or perhaps only one, to see if I can get a little bit of help. Wish me luck."

With that, Emily pushed herself up off the blanket she'd brought. She groaned a little as her knees popped, wondering why she hadn't brought herself a chair instead. She wasn't getting any younger, and her body seemed determined to remind her of that on a regular basis. That was all right, though. She didn't have to be young or spry. The business that she needed to take care of right now simply required a logical brain and a passionate heart.

2

"Emily, it's always so nice to see you." Detective Constable Alyssa Bradley sat down across from Emily at the Daydream Cafe, a hot cup of coffee in her hands. Her dark hair was pulled back in a low ponytail to accommodate her uniform hat, which she set on the table near the window. Her bright eyes sparkled. "I feel like it's been a little while."

"I think it has," Emily agreed. She'd ordered a large hot tea and had treated herself to a pastry. Most of the time, she tried not to let herself indulge too much. There were always plenty of tasty looking goodies here at the café, but she only had to inhale their scent to make her clothes fit more tightly. Today, however, was different. Today, she wanted to spoil herself. "How are things going with work?"

"Very well, thank you," Alyssa replied with a smile. "Chief Inspector Woods has actually started taking me seriously. At first, he didn't always want to hear what I had to say regarding a case."

"I can imagine," Emily murmured. She'd met the man a couple of times. On her first meeting with him, she had just found a dead body in an alley. Woods had treated her kindly, though he'd been incredibly condescending due to her age. The next time they'd met, he didn't seem to remember her at all. He had his work to do, and he didn't want anyone to interfere with it. In a way, Emily understood. The public needed to let the police do their job. But Emily also knew that the numerous cases she'd helped solve would never have gone anywhere if Alyssa hadn't been there to pass along the information.

"Yes, I know." Alyssa made a face as she thought about her boss. "He doesn't mean to be that way. He's been in the business for a long time, though, and I guess you get a bit jaded after a while. It's easy for him to think that young officers are trying to show off, even if we genuinely care about the case and about justice."

"But you said he's noticed you?" Emily prompted. She knew of Alyssa's dreams to be chief inspector herself one day, and she certainly hoped it happened.

"Yes. He's been putting me on better cases, for one thing. When he asks for an update, he appears to listen to what I have to say, and he doesn't go back and check my work as much. Not that I minded when he ran over everything with a fine-toothed comb. I'd much rather have a boss who's detail oriented and wants to get everything right instead of someone who merely brushes it all off like it doesn't matter."

Emily took a bite of her pastry. The glaze on the outside cracked off perfectly, exposing the soft crush. The apple filling was the best part, all cinnamon and sweetness. "I'm very happy for you," she said when she'd finished chewing.

"Thank you, and I truly am grateful to you. I know I wouldn't be where I am if it hadn't been for your help," Alyssa replied. "You're quite the sleuth yourself, Emily."

"I don't know about that," Emily said demurely. "I think it's that you have a different perspective when you get to be as old as dirt."

Alyssa laughed as she took a sip of her coffee, clapping her hand over her mouth to keep herself from making a mess. "You certainly are not!" she chastised when she'd recovered. "You've got plenty of sleuthing years left in you."

"Well, I'd like to hope so." Emily fingered the pendant around her neck, wondering if Alyssa was right. If she was, then she would have to do this. She'd just have to.

"Speaking of, I suppose that's why I haven't seen you in a while," Alyssa concluded. "You haven't had any murders or burglaries to look into lately. Or have you?" The young detective leaned back and eyed Emily, waiting for the news to come.

"No," Emily admitted. "I haven't come across any fresh corpses, and I don't know of any missing paintings or other stolen items. I do think, however, that there's something you might be able to help me with." Nerves slithered in her stomach. She'd only told one other person what she wanted to do, but Anita hardly counted. The two of them had been friends for so long that they practically shared a brain. Everything that Emily knew, Anita knew as well.

Alyssa pushed her coffee mug to the side and leaned forward over the table. She'd been happy and relaxed, but now her face grew serious. It changed her completely, making her go from a carefree girl to a very intense woman. It was a fascinating dichotomy, and Emily thought that was probably exactly what made the girl so good at her job. Alyssa had a true passion for shedding light on the truth. "What's wrong, Emily?"

Emily pulled in a deep breath. No matter how many times she'd rehearsed this conversation in her head, she hadn't been able to find quite the right way to say it. "That's exactly what I'm trying to figure out. I told you about my late husband?"

"Yes, a few times."

Emily ran her hand down the chain around her neck until she reached the pendant. She lifted it up over her head and held the St. Elmo's medal out so that Alyssa could see it. "This was Sebastian's. It was his good luck charm, something that he took with him every time he went boating. You see, when he was a little boy, his grandfather took him out sailing for the first time. The weather changed abruptly, and the wind was whipping them around. Sebastian didn't think they'd ever make it back to dry land again, but his grandfather was an old sailor who'd been through all kinds of storms. He knew things would be all right, but he also understood how terrifying it was not to believe that. He took this off and gave it to Sebastian, explaining that sailors use it to bring them good luck when they're out on the water. Sebastian took it with him every time he went out after that."

Alyssa touched a finger to the small, raised figure with a ship in the background. "Didn't you say he died in a boating accident?"

"That last word is the one I've been having trouble with lately," Emily admitted. "Sebastian wasn't the kind to take risks. I mean, he was an insurance adjuster. It was a part of his personality. Even with his good luck charm, he would never go out if there was a chance of a storm or if something was wrong with the boat.

The young officer regarded her for a long moment. "You're telling me that you don't think your husband's death was an accident."

It was a statement and not a question, which Emily truly appreciated. She'd known Alyssa would be the right person to go to, someone who would believe her without question instead of waving her off as a silly old woman. "I couldn't believe it when I received the call that he'd fallen off the boat and into rough water. I thought they might have even called the wrong house at first. They weren't able to find him for a while. I think, if they never had, then I might still believe he was out there alive somewhere. I suppose there's some relief in that, but it's no real relief to have your husband's body pulled from the bay."

"Oh, Emily." Alyssa reached out and laid her hand gently over Emily's on the table. "I'm so sorry."

"Thank you." Emily pressed her lips together, willing the tears that burned at the backs of her eyes to go away. She could cry later if she needed to. She'd certainly had her share of tears ever since the accident. But right now, this was something she had to do, and she didn't want her emotions to get in the way. "I asked you here to see if you would help me find out more information about his death. I want to know for sure if this was an accident, because I think it very well may have been murder."

Alyssa took a deep breath and let it out slowly while she thought. "It's not going to be an easy thing. You'll be dredging through a lot of old memories. I'll have to talk to you about everything you remember, and then we'll undoubtedly talk about the same things several more times. You'll probably feel like you're reliving some of those days."

"I understand." And she did. Emily knew that this investigation, if there was going to be one, would mostly center around her. She was the one who wanted to know, and she knew more about Sebastian than anyone else. "I'm prepared for it. I think that might be what I've been preparing for this entire time."

The gentleness was returning to Alyssa's face as her detective's mask slipped. "Maybe so. I think you've got more experience than a lot of folks do. But really, Emily. It's going to be terribly hard on you."

She had been nervous, but now true fear gripped her throat. "Are you saying you won't help me?" Emily asked.

"No, that's not what I'm saying at all," Alyssa quickly reassured her as she squeezed her hand. "I'm truly going to be worried about you."

Emily shook her head. "Don't you bother with that. I can worry about myself just fine, and if it's not enough, then I'll have Anita do it."

This earned her a bit of a laugh from Alyssa. "Fair enough."

While Emily had put her nose in the middle of several other cases, this one felt entirely different. She wasn't a witness, and she hadn't found a body. In those cases, things were a little more automatic. This one was already different, and so she thought she knew what Alyssa meant. "Where do we start?"

"From the very beginning." Alyssa took a slim laptop out of her bag. "Tell me everything you know."

3

"I see you looking at me that way. You're being judgy. But I can do this." Emily shook her finger at the cat. "I may be an old lady, but it's not as though I don't still have some life in me yet."

Rosemary sat on the foot of the bed, watching Emily with her big gold eyes. When her owner got a little bit closer, she flopped down on her side and stretched out one fluffy paw.

"You can be as cute as you want to and try to make me want to stay home, but it simply won't work." Emily, unable to resist completely, stroked her hand down the cat's back before crossing the room to check her hair in the mirror. It was an atrocious mess as it always was, with her red-gray curls spiraling everywhere. The various bottles, tubes, tubs, and cans on her dresser were the evidence that she'd tried many different ways to tame it, but nothing ever seemed to work for long. At this point, she'd decided that it was easier to embrace it than to fight it.

Rosemary hopped off the bed and came over to twirl delicately around Emily's legs, making sure to caress her tail fluff on her owner's calves.

"Is that reassurance?" Emily asked, bending down and swooping the cat up into her arms. "A vote of confidence? Well then, I suppose I should take it, if it comes from you. I need someone to believe in me. Now, don't get me wrong. I know Anita is all for this. She's been nothing less than supportive. The children, well, they don't even know. I plan to keep it that way for now, so don't you tell them."

The cat gently pressed her cold nose against Emily's.

"That's my girl."

A car horn blew outside, startling them both.

"That'll be Alyssa," Emily announced, putting Rosemary back on the bed. "You be a good girl and mind the house. I won't be long. Actually, I don't know if that's true or not. I might be, depending on what Alyssa has planned after our first meeting. Anyway, I don't know. Just be good."

Slipping on her shoes and grabbing her handbag, Emily trotted out and got in the passenger's side of Alyssa's squad car. She tried to ignore all the extra electronics attached to the dashboard to make it into a police vehicle, squirming around the laptop as she put her seatbelt on. "It was kind of you to pick me up, but I hope it wasn't an inconvenience."

"Not at all, and I thought it made sense since we need to go back to the station." Alyssa put the car in reverse and slowly backed out of the driveway.

"Yes. That station." Emily's nerves had returned. "I have to admit, I wish we didn't have to discuss this with Chief Inspector Woods."

"I know," Alyssa sympathized. "To be honest, I'd also rather not have to. I'd like to keep my job, though, and this is the right thing to do. We'll go in and explain things. He's a reasonable man, and then we'll know we're not sneaking around behind his back."

It was all very sensible, but Emily found a jumping feeling in her stomach that had been returning to her quite a bit lately. She still hadn't shaken it by the time they got downtown and were seated in Woods' office side by side.

"All right." Woods came in and closed the door behind him before taking a seat at his desk. "What's this all about, then?"

"I believe my husband was murdered," Emily began.

"You *believe?*" Woods asked. He looked over at Alyssa. "What is this all about?"

"Sebastian Cherry was killed in a boating accident a few years ago," she began.

"An accident?" he interrupted, his brow raised.

Emily hadn't liked the idea of coming here. She knew what this man was like. Already, she could hear the disdain in his voice.

"That's how it was ruled initially," Alyssa admitted. "Some other information that has come to light recently has made his widow think the opposite might be true."

Looking at them each in turn, Chief Inspector Woods picked up his phone. He muttered into it for a moment and hung up. "I think I'm going to need some more information."

Alyssa had warned her about this, so Emily had done her best to prepare. She gave a very simplified version of the events that had happened on that fateful day, when Sebastian had been asked to go out on an impromptu boating trip with some new friends of his. "They did rule it as an accident at the time," she admitted, "but I don't think that can be true."

Woods' eyes lifted toward the ceiling but then he forced them back down to look at her. Emily got the distinct feeling he had stopped himself in the middle of rolling his eyes. No doubt, he heard stories like this on a regular basis.

That was all right. He'd just have to hear hers, too. "You see, there are several things that I've realized since then that make me think this might not have been an accident at all."

"Such as?" he prompted, tapping a pencil's eraser end on the edge of his desk.

Emily noticed he wasn't taking any notes, but she tried to ignore that for the moment. She knew that she and Alyssa had plenty of notes for all of them. "For instance, there's a man who keeps coming to visit Sebastian's grave in the cemetery. I have no idea who he is. When I tried to chat with him, he said he would come to walk and that he would visit all sorts of graves, but I've only ever seen him visit my husband." As she told him, Emily become more and more sure that there was something about his mysterious man that tied in with Sebastian's death. She'd seen him several times at the graveyard, and that in itself seemed like an interesting coincidence.

A knock sounded on the door, and a young clerk stepped in to hand Inspector Woods a file. "Thank you," the man grumbled as the door shut again behind the clerk.

Emily could see right away that this was the file on the boating accident. Her heart clutched inside her chest. Alyssa had been right. This was all a lot more real than she thought it would be. It was one thing to figure out who had killed a young waiter that she didn't know or who stole funds from a craft fair. Those were personal in that she felt she was involved, but they weren't this personal.

Inspector Woods flicked through a few pages before he closed it again. His dark brows were ominously close together as he turned to Alyssa. "DC Bradley, you know full well that the department doesn't have the time or the manpower to go back and open a case that's already been closed without a very solid reason. I'm afraid a hunch, a feeling, or even a mysterious man at cemetery isn't solid enough."

The top of Alyssa's tongue flicked out to touch the corner of her mouth. "I understand that it might not look like it on the surface, sir, but there are actually several other things that make this a case worth looking back into."

His mouth was a hard line. "You're welcome to put together a memo and submit it to me, but I'll tell you right now that this is extremely unlikely. I wasn't even the inspector at the time that this case happened, and I don't want someone to think I'm going back to make sure my predecessor did his job. Like I said, not unless there is a very strong reason to do so. It's not practical for us on numerous levels."

"I understand, sir. I'll submit that memo as soon as possible."

He gave her a curt nod. "That will be all. It's nice to see you, Mrs. Cherry."

With that, they were dismissed.

Emily felt as though the weight of the world was on her shoulders as they walked back outside. The beautiful spring sunshine beckoned the people of Little Oakley to come out for a jog or to take their children to the park, but Emily felt dark and gloomy as they made their way through the parking lot. "I suppose that's it, then. It's over before it's even done."

Alyssa paused with her fingers on the doorhandle. She looked at Emily. "I wouldn't say that."

Once inside the vehicle, Emily turned to her as she got her seatbelt on. "What do you mean? Inspector Woods said that he doesn't want to do it."

"Yes, but he also said that I can put together a memo making my case and submit it to him," Alyssa pointed out. "I'll be doing that this afternoon."

Emily frowned. "Even so, it sounded as though he was only going through the motions so he could feel like he did the right thing. He's not going to reopen the case." Sadness gripped her, and she tried to fight it off. Nothing would change the fact that Sebastian was gone, whether she had a chance to look into his death or not.

Alyssa ran her tongue over her teeth as she leaned back in her seat. She looked out over the parking lot, but her eyes were different. "Have you heard of those true crime podcasters who go back and look at the evidence in old cases?"

"My friend Toby has a podcast." It was the first thing that came to her mind, since the young man at the grocery store had eagerly told her how he was putting his new recording equipment to work. "He talks about music and local bands, though. I don't know much about the other ones."

"They're pretty popular, and you might like them. Anyway, sometimes they're able to put together enough clues to find a killer or to have an innocent man released from prison. If they can do that on their own without any police assistance, then I don't see why we can't." Alyssa fired up the engine.

Emily looked around her at the very real police car she was sitting in at the moment. "But you're not a podcaster. If you go after this case without Inspector Woods' permission, you might lose your job. I can't have that."

Alyssa put her hand on the shifter knob. "You know, I chose this line of work because I was interested in the truth. I'm the kind of person who absolutely believes rules should be followed, but not if they keep you from the truth. Now let's go see what we can find out." She put the car in drive and headed out of the lot.

4

T he salty air and the call of gulls filled Emily's senses, but her stomach churned a little at the thought of being back here. She and Alyssa walked along the docks, their footsteps thumping on the wooden boards. "You know, I'm only now realizing that I haven't been to the ocean once since Sebastian died."

"That makes sense," Alyssa replied sagely. It was her day off work, and she had traded her uniform for a yellow button-down blouse and khaki trousers. It was almost strange to see her in street clothes, but she looked nice.

"I don't know that it really does when I live in a town so close to the sea. I haven't even taken my granddaughters out here. I suppose my daughter and her husband have, and it's not as though I have some sort of obligation to make sure they go to the beach. I never noticed how much I was avoiding it. And now I see how much I'm babbling."

Emily felt heated prickles all over her skin. She wasn't really embarrassed, not in front of someone like Alyssa, whom she knew so well. It was just so odd to be back here, as though she had woken up and found herself still in a nightmare.

"People handle things differently when something traumatic happens to them." Alyssa put her hands in her pockets as they walked past the boat slips. "Sometimes they want to come back to the place where it happened or keep some other reminder around because it lets them know how far they've come. Other times, they put it in the past and keep it there. It doesn't mean that either way is necessarily wrong, as long as it's working for them."

"You're very wise for your age. Did I ever tell you that?" Emily could feel her curls tightening in the humid air, and she was glad that she'd caught them back in a kerchief for the day.

Alyssa laughed. "I wouldn't say that. It's that I've attended some group counseling sessions for victims of crimes. It's part of our training for the department, so we can understand the people we're dealing with in the community."

Emily raised her brows. "That's very forward thinking. I'm glad to hear it. Oh, my." Her footsteps slowed and then stopped.

"This is it?"

She nodded. She'd only seen it once, but Emily wasn't about to forget *The Sincerity*. The yacht was one that Sebastian had called small, though it had to be at least fifty feet long. It had a bridge on the top that looked out over the water, and small porthole windows that led to the living quarters below. These things were rather luxurious, from what she understood.

"It's been far too long for there to be any real kind of evidence or clues," Alyssa explained as they walked a little bit closer, "but I thought it would be a good idea to have a clear picture of where everything happened. It can help give us a frame of reference."

Emily looked at all that smooth white fiberglass, shining so pristinely in the sun. Her eyes focused on the sturdy railing that ran all around the deck. "It's odd. He fell over the side of the boat, but that meant he'd have to go over the railing. Otherwise, he'd have to be at the back of the boat. I don't think there would be any reason for him to be back there."

"Mmm." Alyssa tapped her chin. "If Inspector Woods clears us, then we'll have access to the file, and we can see what the witnesses said. It may not be helpful at all, but that's at least one aspect we can look into."

"Speaking of witnesses..." Something had made Emily look off to her right, though she couldn't say what. She spotted a couple walking out on the dock, wearing brightly colored clothing and hats, clearly ready for a day out in the sun.

"You know them?" Alyssa looked, trying not to be obvious.

"They own the boat," Emily managed to get out just before the couple noticed they were standing there.

Their footsteps slowed down as they approached. "Hello, there," the woman said as they approached. "Can we help you with something?"

She was smiling and looking at them good-naturedly, but Emily's shoulders felt tight. She'd thought Alyssa's idea to look at the boat was a good idea, but now she wished they hadn't. "Oh, no. I'm sorry. It's been a while, but we've met before. My name is Emily Cherry."

"Emily Cherry," the woman repeated as she shook Emily's hand. The smile slowly faded from her face as she realized to whom she was talking. "Oh."

"My aunt and I were out for a walk, and since the boat was right here, we decided to stop for a moment," Alyssa explained with a smile and a breathy laugh. "We didn't mean to disturb you or keep you from your day. I'm Alyssa, by the way."

"Oh, yes." Emily hadn't made any introductions, but now she was glad she hadn't. It would've been difficult to introduce Alyssa without that excuse. "This is Dillon and Annie Dixon. They own *The Sincerity*."

"It's a beautiful boat. I understand they're absolutely gorgeous inside." Alyssa looked at the yacht and sighed. "Someday, right?"

If she'd hoped to get an invitation on deck, Dillon wasn't biting. "It's nice to see you again, Mrs. Cherry. And it's nice to meet you, Alyssa. Annie and I really have to get going, though. Please excuse us." He gestured at his wife, putting his hand on the small of her back and guiding her to the gangway.

Slowly, pretending that they had nothing better to do, Emily and Alyssa resumed their walk down the docks.

"An interesting couple," Alyssa said when they were out of earshot.

Emily nodded. "That was a nice cover you came up with, and quickly, too. I'm afraid I'm good at making things awkward for them."

"What do you mean?" They moved into an area where the slips were smaller, holding shorter boats that were more affordable.

"I ran into them a while back at a party at the country club," Emily explained. "Maybe I should've left them alone, but they were the last ones to see Sebastian alive. I suppose I thought I would get some sort of closure by going over and introducing myself. Like today, Dillon made excuses about needing to leave. I can't say that I blame him. I wouldn't want to spend any time with me if I were in their position."

Alyssa turned away from the water and toward a walkway that would bring them back to the parking lot. "You're blaming yourself too much. Yes, it's awkward, but that doesn't mean it always has to be avoided. How did Sebastian know these people?"

The sea breeze tried to yank Emily's hair out of its containment, but she tucked it firmly back underneath her kerchief as she thought. "You know, I have no idea. He may have told me, but I don't remember." She racked her brain, thinking that the information must be in there somewhere. It was likely erased by the tragedy of Sebastian's death.

"Dillon Dixon, right?" Alyssa had her phone out now.

"Yes, and Annie. She seems very nice. She looked like she genuinely wanted to help us as she walked up. I suppose there might be other folks coming out here to look for a specific boat and needing help."

"Possibly," Alyssa muttered, but she was swiping away at her phone screen. "Hm."

"What is it?"

"Not much, or maybe not anything at all. I was curious what I could find out about the Dixons online, other than the fact that they own a yacht. Looks like he's the CEO of a place called Vertex Financial."

Emily shrugged. "I can't say that I've heard of it."

Alyssa's thumbs continued to work as they walked. "Me, neither, but the internet knows everything. It's a relatively new company, and it looks like they specialize in investments and portfolio management, things like that."

"I suppose that's how he managed to buy a fancy boat like that." Emily and Sebastian had always been careful with their finances, and it meant that she was able to live a comfortable retirement, not on a yacht, but comfortable.

"Does the company name mean anything to you?" Alyssa asked, still scrolling through her phone.

"No, I don't think so."

"Okay. I wish I could've talked to them a little more, but I don't see a good way to do that right now, not until we get approval from Woods. I think we will, though." Alyssa put her phone away and straightened her shoulders as she continued toward the car.

Emily wasn't so sure.

5

"This is our next stop. How are you holding up?"

"Fine," Emily replied quickly. She glanced over to see Alyssa giving her a long and studious look. "I really am. Don't start getting all patronizing like everyone else on the planet just because I'm an old woman."

"I'm sorry," Alyssa replied as she pulled the car over into a slot. "I worry about you. I've come to think of you as part of my family, and I know this isn't easy."

She'd said that a lot, but probably because it was true. "The important things never are. Besides, coming to the cemetery is something I do on a regular basis. I'm here all the time, so this is nothing new. I'll admit that going to see the boat was a little unsettling, but I'll be fine."

"Okay."

"Are you my niece here, too?" Emily asked as she unbuckled her seatbelt.

"I suppose that depends on who run into," Alyssa replied with a grin.

The cemetery was quiet and peaceful, the only background noise being the gentle hum of distant traffic and a few birds singing in the trees. "Isn't it funny?" Emily asked as she automatically made her way to Sebastian's grave. "We make such beautiful places for the dead, but we don't always do the same for ourselves while we're alive."

"Are you saying I should plant some flowers in front of my house?" Alyssa smiled. "You don't think plain concrete and mud are attractive?"

Emily laughed, knowing that Alyssa was a busy young woman and hardly had any time for things like landscaping. "To each their own, I suppose, but maybe I'll buy you some lily bulbs as a spring present. Or maybe I'll come and stick them in the ground when you're not home, and you'll be surprised when they come up."

"Make sure they're bright red, so I know they're from you," the detective teased.

"Here we are." Emily gestured to the familiar headstone.

Alyssa studied it for a moment, but then she scanned the entirety of the surrounding cemetery. "How often would you say you saw this man?"

"I wish I'd taken note so I could tell you more accurately. I come here about once a week, and I'd say I've seen him a handful of times. I didn't always really pay attention, you know. I was more focused on what I was here to do. I think I'd seen him a couple of times before that time I told you about where he seemed to be visiting Sebastian. Oh, I don't think I'm making sense anymore." Emily flapped her hand in the air in frustration.

"Yes, you are. Don't worry about it. I know these things aren't always easy to describe, and don't forget that the kinds of conversations we've been having are what I do all the time. I talk to rattled witnesses who wish they'd paid more attention because they didn't realize at the time that there was anything to pay attention to. I get it." Alyssa put a soothing hand on Emily's arm.

The afternoon light slanted down through the trees. Emily clasped her hands in front of her as she looked down at Sebastian's name, letters that she had traced with her fingers so many times over the last few years. If only he were able to tell them what had really happened. He was the one who knew, and Emily hoped she could find out the truth, not only for her own sake, but also for his.

"Where's the office?"

Emily pointed off toward the south entrance. "Over there, I believe."

"Let's go."

They moved carefully through the graves, making sure not to step in the wrong spot. Noticing a bouquet that was drooping dangerously out of its vase, Emily stopped to fix it.

"Thanks!"

Emily started at the voice. She automatically looked down at the gravestone, but feeling foolish, she turned to see than an older gentleman was working a short distance away.

He held a long pair of loppers and was carefully trimming a small tree. He took off his cap, revealing a head of wispy gray hair, and waved it. "You're making my job that much easier," he said with a grin.

"Oh." Recovering, Emily realized that she'd seen him here before. She'd always been so preoccupied with Sebastian that she didn't often notice. "You're the groundskeeper, aren't you?"

"Yes, ma'am. Hugo Williams, at your service." He pressed his cap to his chest as he bent forward in an extravagant vow that was quite the contrast to his muddy coveralls. "Do you ladies need help with anything? I've been working here for pretty much my entire adult life, so I've got the whole place mapped out in my brain." He pointed one finger at his temple for emphasis.

"Yes, actually." Alyssa had taken the lead back at the boat docks, but Emily had been overwhelmed at that moment. Here, she was really quite comfortable. "We were looking for some information on someone who comes here a lot."

"Hm, well, I'll do my best. Most folks don't pay much attention to me unless they get lost. My daily conversations are with the tenants, and they don't really talk back much." Hugo chuckled as he pointed to the nearest tombstone.

Emily knew she needed to do a better job of describing exactly who she was talking about. "He's rather tall, and I've usually seen him wearing a gray overcoat. His sedan is gray, as well."

"All that gray, are you sure he's not a ghost?" Hugo cracked.

"I'm pretty certain," Emily replied with a smile, reasoning that working in a place like this was bound to give a man like Hugo an interesting sense of humor. "He has short dark hair, blue eyes, and a very square jawline. And an aquiline nose," she added, proud of herself that even if she couldn't recall enough details about when she'd seen him, she hadn't forgotten his face.

"Goodness, is he a man or a movie star?" Hugo slapped his knee and laughed at his own joke. "I do think I've seen him here before. Comes by fairly regularly, usually heads over there to the back quadrant."

Emily's heart jumped up in her chest as she felt like they were making some sort of progress. "Do you know who he's here to see?"

Hugo's pale eyes winked in the sunlight. "He didn't exactly make reservations, you know."

Alyssa pulled her badge out of her pocket and flashed it briefly. "Mr. Williams, if there's any information you could give us, we'd greatly appreciate it."

His eyes went wide as he settled his cap on his head. He set the pair of loppers down, letting them lean against the tree, and then he readjusted his hat again. "Say, what's this all about, anyway?"

Alyssa's face was serious, but not unkind. "I'm afraid I'm not at liberty to disclose the details to you at the moment."

"Oh, my." Hugo swallowed, looking a bit panicked. "I don't want to cause any trouble."

Emily could see that Alyssa's badge had scared the man, and she couldn't help but feel a little sorry for him. "There's no trouble at all," she assured him with a smile, imagining what ideas must be running through his mind as he tried to sort out why a young woman with a badge and an old lady would be here asking him questions. "There's someone we're looking for, and we understand the comes here often."

"Yes." He swallowed again, but he looked a little steadier now. "He does."

"Do you happen to know his name or when he visits?" Alyssa pressed gently.

"I don't. I'm afraid graveyards don't have guestbooks!" Hugo was back to his normal self, laughing at his own joke. The glare in Alyssa's eye made him quickly stop chuckling, and he once again rearranged his hat on his head as he cleared his throat.

"Are there any types of records kept? Or video surveillance?" Alyssa asked. She had changed her countenance, realizing she'd scared the man. "Anything you can provide would be helpful."

Hugo shook his head. "I'm afraid not, ma'am. The only records we keep are of those who are buried here and where they are. We haven't had any trouble with vandalism, so we haven't put up any cameras like some of the other cemeteries have. It's pretty peaceful, really, and that's one of the reasons I like it." He gave a tentative smile.

"You do a wonderful job of keeping it up," Emily said, not wanting the poor man to feel discouraged. "I come every week to visit my husband, and there's never a weed in sight. I have to say, I appreciate the flower beds, too."

"Do you?" He straightened a little and grinned. "I planted all of those myself, you know. Folks come and leave flowers for their loved ones, of course, but those only last so long. I noticed that when I started working here, and I thought it would be nice to have some pretty landscaping all year long. I've tried to put a nice mix in each bed so that there are flowers from spring to fall and plenty of greenery in the winter."

Alyssa reached back into her pocket, but this time she took out a business card instead of a badge. "You've done a wonderful job, Mr. Williams. If you could give me a call the next time you see the man we described, I'd greatly appreciate it."

"Of course. Of course." He took the card and studied it for a moment before putting it in the chest pocket of his coveralls and patting it into place. "The man in gray. I surely will."

"Thank you very much." Emily led the way back to the car, feeling the tension in her shoulders slowly ease. "I think you scared the dickens out of him."

"I didn't mean to. I really didn't." Alyssa grimaced, looking guilty. "My mother always told me that my face said everything my mouth didn't. I was getting tired of his jokes, and I guess it showed."

"Well, no real harm done. He seems nice enough, and even though he didn't have anything to tell us today, maybe we'll get a call from him soon." Emily wondered how long it would be. She'd seen the mysterious man less than a week ago. Would they have to wait a few days, a couple of weeks, or a month? Oh, how she wished she'd paid more attention!

"He's chatty enough that I'm sure he won't mind," Alyssa said with a laugh.

6

"Come on inside and I'll fix you something to eat," Emily insisted when Alyssa pulled up in front of her house.

"I can't let you do that. You must be exhausted," Alyssa insisted.

Emily couldn't deny that was true. They'd made a few stops, and it was only the very beginning of their investigation. Alyssa had said it was important to set the scene, something that Emily agreed with. Any clues they might find wouldn't make any sense without context. And yet it had been utterly draining to not only talk about Sebastian all day but to visit the places that were the more essential to the last part of his life.

"I am," she admitted, "but I learned a long time ago that there are some things you have to do no matter how tired you feel. Eating is one of them."

"I never said I wouldn't eat," Alyssa countered, "just that I don't want you to go to the trouble of cooking for me."

"Well then you can help me go through some leftovers," Emily insisted. "I still tend to cook as though I have a husband and three children at home, and I certainly get tired of having the same thing night after night. We can find something to warm up."

"I don't know." Alyssa drummed her fingers on the steering wheel.

"What will you eat if you don't come in?" Emily challenged.

"Probably something terrible for me in a greasy paper bag." Alyssa laughed as she turned off the car. "Fine. You've talked me into it."

"I suppose I'm good at that, since I've already talked you into this investigation." Emily unlocked the door and automatically looked for Rosemary. The fluffy cat usually came running to greet her, but this time she was nowhere in sight. That was odd.

Alyssa slipped out of her shoes and left them near the door. "You didn't exactly have to convince me. I mean, you want to know what really happened to your husband. It's a big deal to you, and I wasn't going to leave you in the lurch. I'm happy to help in any way that I can. Goodness knows, you've certainly been helping me."

"Oh, that's not much," Emily said as she stepped over to the end of the couch to see if Rosemary had curled up near the bookshelf where she sometimes liked to nap. "To be honest with you, part of me hopes that we don't find anything at all."

"I think that's understandable. Even though you have your suspicions, it's easier to think that Sebastian died because of an accident."

Emily smiled at her. Alyssa's story about being her niece was something she'd made up, but the young detective really was like family to her. "Yes. Exactly. Now let's find something to eat."

She stepped into the kitchen and froze. They weren't alone. She felt the eyes watching her even before she slowly turned to her right to look at the attached dining room. Her entire family was standing around the table, which was groaning with big plates of food. A large cake sat in the middle. The lights were off, but Emily managed to find the switch and turned them on. "What on earth?"

"Hello, Mother," Nathan said stiffly, his eyes darting back and forth between Emily and Alyssa. "We came to surprise you."

"You definitely did that. But why? It's not my birthday or anything." For reasons she couldn't quite fathom, they all looked as shocked as she felt.

Mavis was standing at the end of the table, near a chair where Rosemary and Gus were both sitting proudly. "We'd all noticed you'd been a bit down lately, but I suppose now we all know why."

Emily covered her mouth with her fingers as she realized that they'd all been standing in here while she and Alyssa had discussed Sebastian's death, their father's potential murder. Her cheeks flushed and her eyes widened, but she didn't quite know what to say.

Phoebe looked at her with concern. "Do you really think Dad was murdered?"

Her throat and chest were tight. Emily pressed her lips together for a moment, trying to gather her thoughts. "I've been wondering, yes," she finally replied.

"Why didn't you tell us?" Genevieve asked gently, her manicured hand firmly secured around her husband's arm.

At least that was an answer she already knew. "I didn't want to bother any of you with it unless I knew for certain. I didn't see a point in raising the alarm when it might turn out to be nothing. I wanted to wait until the time was right, but I hadn't meant for you to find out this way. Oh, goodness. The girls aren't here, are they?" Emily looked around for her granddaughters.

Matthew shook his head. "They couldn't keep their giggles under control for the surprise, so we set them up to play in the guest bedroom. We told them they could give you their own surprise."

"And yet I'm the one who has surprised everyone," Emily concluded, feeling shaky.

"I think you should come and sit down, Mother." Nathan stepped away from the table and guided her toward a chair.

Her son had been coddling her ever since Sebastian had died, worrying and fussing over her like she was a delicate little thing. At times it had driven Emily crazy, but right now she let it happen. She really did need to sit down. "Where are my manners? I don't remember which of you might have already met her, but this is DC Alyssa Bradley. We've come to know each other over the last few years, and she's agreed to help me look into this business with your father."

Nathan raised an eyebrow. "So, this is all sanctioned by the police department? I've always had a feeling that Mother was getting herself into trouble with the way she kept snooping into murders and robberies around town."

Alyssa's eyes held concern for Emily as well as they shared a glance. She didn't explain the past but only concentrated on the present. "We're still waiting on the final approval from Chief Inspector Woods. At the moment, Emily and I have been going over what she remembers and trying to make sure we have all the details in order."

It wasn't a lie. Only Hugo Williams had any idea that this was police business, and Emily didn't think he was the type to call up the department and verify that what they were doing was legitimate.

Mavis sat down and pulled Gus into her lap. "You know, I've always wondered how Dad could possibly have had a boating accident. He was the most careful man I'd ever met, both on land and at sea."

"That's true," Phoebe agreed. "Remember how he always had a change of clothes and emergency supplies in the trunk, even when he was only driving across town?"

"And when we were little, it was practically an entire suitcase, to make sure he had all of us taken care of," Nathan said with a shake of his head. "I thought it was kind of embarrassing for a long time, but not when I slipped in the mud, and he was right there with an extra change of clothes."

It was sweet to hear them reminiscing so fondly, but Emily knew what was coming next. Nathan would tell her that this was far too dangerous, and Phoebe would come up with some other way for Emily to occupy her time. They now knew what she was up to and would undoubtedly try to stop her.

Mavis was the only one she was uncertain about, and right now her youngest was regarding her with genuine concern on her face. "Mom, is there anything we can do to help?"

Emily's heart leapt up in her throat. "Really?"

She gave a little shrug. "Of course. I've been a little bit of a help to you in these cases before, and I'd like to do what I can."

"So will I," Phoebe said before Emily had a chance to reply. "I mean, I have the girls to take care of, but I'm here for it anyway."

Matthew's brows raised in surprise, but he simply nodded. He was always a very calm man, and he would never deny Phoebe something she truly wanted.

Slowly, Emily's eyes locked with Nathan's. Her son was a strong and stubborn man. It had earned him a good career and a marriage that made him happy, but it meant that the two of them had often butted heads. Emily lifted her chin and straightened her shoulders, knowing exactly what to expect from him. He would try to talk her out of it, just as he did any other time she was doing something that he thought might be too dangerous, but he wouldn't be successful. This was a truth she absolutely had to find.

Nathan looked at his sisters each in turn and then Alyssa. When he looked back down at Emily, he smiled a little. "You're the one in charge, Mother. I don't know a thing about solving mysteries. You tell me what to do."

"Oh, you dear sweet things!" Emily pulled her three children into her arms, waving Genevieve, Matthew, and Alyssa into the embrace as well. "I love you all so much, and I can't tell you how much it means to me to have your support in this."

When they straightened up, Emily felt a tickle at her ankle. She looked down to see Rosemary winding herself around Emily's leg. "Yes, you too," Emily laughed as she scooped the cat up into her arms. "You've been here for the whole journey. Now let's you and I go to the guest bedroom and let Lucy and Ella surprise me. You can act surprised, too."

As she made her way down the hall, Emily felt a frisson of energy running through her heart. When Nathan had come into the world and made her a mother, she'd known what she wanted to do. She'd wanted to have a close, loving family, the kind that would get together even after everyone had moved off in their own directions and that would support each other no matter what. And now, regardless of what happened with Sebastian's case, she knew she'd at least done that.

7

Emily tried to keep herself calmly seated while she waited, although she wanted to get up and pace the room while Alyssa read through Sebastian's journal entries. The one that Emily had found that'd seemed most relevant was a short one, but Emily had agreed that Alyssa should look through several other passages to see if there was anything of interest. Emily herself had already gone through the little book, so she knew there was nothing more embarrassing inside than a few sweet comments about how much Sebastian loved her. Still, she was desperate to know what Alyssa thought.

"Hm." Alyssa closed the book and ran her tongue over her teeth.

"Hm, what?" Rosemary was on her lap, and Emily took advantage of it by stroking her fingers through the thick fur. It gave her something to do.

"I don't have to tell you that Sebastian was worried about something with his work."

Emily nodded. It was that entry that described his concerns that'd made Emily wonder what was going on at the end of Sebastian's life that he hadn't told her about. He hadn't wanted to worry her, but it *did* bother her that he'd never mentioned anything. She and Sebastian had been incredibly close, and they'd even worked for the same company. It was very odd.

Alyssa set the journal aside and flipped open the notebook she was using to keep track of their investigation. "You mentioned that you had found a claim form from the same company."

"Yes." Emily remembered it clearly, because it had been so odd to her at the time. "I'm assuming it must have slipped out from the company's file, which he mentioned in his journal that he was going to bring home."

"And you and Sebastian both worked for Phoenix Insurance, correct?"

"That's right. That's where we met, actually." Emily had to smile a little at the memory. The job itself hadn't been anything particularly exciting, but knowing what it'd brought into her life had always made her rather satisfied with it.

"And what do you know about this Dorris Financial?"

Emily rolled her eyes up toward the ceiling as she thought. "Not a whole lot, really. Sebastian and I worked in different departments, and we did our best not to bring our work home with us in the evenings. I do know—as everyone else did who worked there—that Dorris had their fleet vehicles insured with us, and they were constantly getting into accidents. I suppose being good with money doesn't necessarily make you a good driver."

"And the claim form?" Alyssa asked hopefully.

"I returned it to Phoenix when I temped there a while back. I admit I was going to slip it back into their file, figuring nobody would be the wiser. I didn't want anyone to know that Sebastian had it at home. But I couldn't find the file, and someone in the records department told me it was being stored off-site because Phoenix didn't do business with Dorris anymore. In fact, I think he even said the company had gone under." She had been a little rattled in the moment, mostly because she'd lied and said she'd found the form in a drawer there at the office.

Alyssa was making notes. She had tiny, neat handwriting that she could produce with remarkable speed. "And did you make a copy of this form?"

"No." She wished now that she had, although she hadn't thought it relevant at the time. "I know it was a claim form for another one of their wrecked fleet vehicles. Sebastian had written the number five with a question mark after it on the top of the page."

"I think we should go to Phoenix Insurance," Alyssa announced, getting up.

"Do you think they'll tell us anything?" Emily asked, surprised by the notion.

"I don't know, but I'm willing to try. The worst thing they can do is say no."

They went outside and got into Alyssa's private vehicle. She'd explained that she wouldn't use her police cruiser until the case was official, just to be safe. "So, do you think you'll let your children help you with this?" she asked casually as they pulled out onto the road.

That had been heavy on Emily's mind since the surprise dinner the other night. "I'm not sure. I think it's wonderful that they want to, and I don't want to leave them out. Ironically, I don't want any of them to put themselves in danger. They fuss over me, but I can fuss over them just as much."

"They really love you," Alyssa said with a smile. "It was sweet to see how much they care."

"Yes." Emily had been surprised all right, but not in the way they'd imagined. "I think we'll just have to see how this goes. There might be something they can do, but knowing that they're behind me is enough for now."

They arrived at Phoenix Insurance far too soon. Emily realized that Alyssa was a lot bolder in her investigation process than she was. That made sense, of course, but it certainly felt different from when she was doing it on her own. She had visions of immediately being kicked out of the Phoenix office as soon as they arrived.

Fortunately, this was a company that hadn't yet decided to keep things closed off from the public with key cards and such. It was simple to walk right in the front door. The woman at the front desk looked at them expectantly and asked if she could help.

"No, thank you," Emily said with a smile that she hoped looked genuine as they breezed on past. "We know where we're headed."

Though she didn't make any effort to stop them, Emily felt a jolt of adrenaline run through her as they wound their way through the dull gray hallways and past multiple offices. When she'd come in for her temporary job, she'd worked on the north end of the building, just as she had when she'd worked here full time. The administration portion of the building was on the south side, and that was where she guided Alyssa now.

She entered a large open room full of desks slightly spaced apart. The air was filled with the sounds of phones ringing, people talking in low voices, and keyboards clicking. It was easy enough to once again find the desk with a small sign that said 'Records' on the front of it. Emily was fairly sure this was the same man she'd talked to before, the one who had explained to her that the records were no longer kept in this building.

He looked up with a bored glance, but his eyes brightened a bit when he saw Alyssa. He ran a hand over his head and then dropped it quickly when he realized he had very little hair left to adjust. "Hello, ladies. Is there something I can do for you?"

"Yes, I think so. We need to get the files for Dorris Financial," Emily announced.

He looked at Emily as though he hadn't noticed her until now, but now that he did, he no longer knew how he was going to help them. He shrugged. "I can't do much for you on that account. We don't do business with them any longer. Those records aren't stored here."

"Is there some way that we could request them?" Alyssa asked politely.

"Pulling old files out of storage takes the approval of the general manager." The longer he looked at them, the more confused he looked. "Hold on a moment. Do you ladies work here? I don't think I've seen you before."

"You and I have met," Emily corrected, knowing that she sounded much more confident than she really was. "I used to work here, and I've come back as a temp before."

"And you?" he asked Alyssa.

Subtly, so that she wouldn't be flashing it to the entire office, Alyssa lifted her hand out of her pocket so that the top of her badge showed. "Not exactly."

The record keeper, who had never bothered to introduce himself, nearly jumped backward in his chair. Beads of sweat stood out on his forehead. "Well, that's not what I expected. In that case, you'd have to have a subpoena or a search warrant, and then I'd still need approval from the general manager."

"Any information that you could give us would be helpful," Alyssa replied, seemingly unperturbed at the idea that he wasn't able to give them the file. "We need to explore the relationship between Dorris Financial and Phoenix Insurance."

The man swallowed uncomfortably. "Like I said, we don't do business with them anymore. I believe that stopped about the time I started working here, but I've probably already said too much. You'll have to come back with some official court documentation. I could check in with the general manager for you, but I'm quite sure you're going to hear the same thing." He gestured toward his phone.

"No, that's all right. I completely understand, and I admire you for doing your job the way you're supposed to. Thank you for your time." Alyssa turned on her heel.

Emily scrambled to follow her. They didn't speak as they retreated through the building, and Emily felt like she could finally breathe once they were outside again. "That didn't go very well."

"I didn't expect it to be much different, to be honest." Alyssa once again climbed behind the wheel and reached for her seat belt. "They're a relatively big company, or at least big enough that they have certain protocols. They can't simply comply because they've seen a badge."

Emily rubbed at a twinge in her lower back, realizing how much time she'd been spending in a car lately. "I admire you, you know. You could've given him a wink and a flirty smile, and he probably would've done anything you asked."

Alyssa looked doubtful. "That's never been how I've wanted to operate. People who do only make it more difficult to have traditionally male roles, and there are some things that I won't compromise on."

"Good for you," Emily said with a firm nod. Alyssa was so young and strong. Emily had never been the sort of beauty that made men trip over their own tongues to help her, but she did wish that she'd been stronger and bolder in her youth. "It's too bad that we couldn't make any progress here. Dorris Financial is out of business as far as I know, so we can't check with them, either."

Alyssa tapped her fingers thoughtfully on the steering wheel. "Did you see how uncomfortable he got when he saw my badge? It makes me wonder if anyone at Phoenix might've had something to do with Sebastian's death in some way."

Emily lifted her hand to her mouth. "I never thought about that before. I can say that it feels very different than it did when I used to work there. Rather unwelcoming. But I can't imagine why anyone who worked there would want to harm Sebastian. He never bothered anyone, and his coworkers all seemed to like him well enough."

"Still, I don't want to leave any possibility left behind until we know for sure."

8

Emily happily sipped her coffee. The investigation made her rather nervous every now and then, more than any other case that she'd been involved in. It was as hard as Alyssa had said it would be, and yet Emily had woken up that morning feeling confident. They hadn't truly made any headway, or at least not the kind she'd hoped for, but neither one of them had given up yet. Emily knew that had to be a good sign, and she had both Alyssa and her family at her back. Anita, of course, had always been on board with this. She was the first person Emily had told about her suspicions, and she'd also been the first to say she should go for it.

She looked up expectantly when Alyssa stepped into the Daydream Café, but she frowned when she saw the urgent look on the detective constable's face. "We've got a bit of a problem," she said as she slid into the booth, not even stopping at the counter to get coffee or a pastry first.

"What is it?" Emily asked, alarmed. Alyssa had been nothing but calm and cool up until now, but the younger woman genuinely looked worried.

"I just got off the phone with Chief Inspector Woods." Alyssa folded her hands in front of her on the table. "Apparently, the man we spoke to at Phoenix Insurance decided to call the department. He wanted to make sure that what we were doing was legitimate, and that I didn't have a fake badge that I was trying to influence him with."

"Do people do that?" That sounded like the kind of thing that only happened in movies.

"It doesn't really matter. The guy was worried that he was getting scammed, so he called it in. I'm on my way to have a meeting with Woods right now." She pressed her shoulders back, strengthening herself for what was to come.

"I'll go get a lid for my cup, and I'll be right with you," Emily promised.

"No." Alyssa reached out and put a hand on Emily's arm to keep her there. "This is my problem. I knew I was breaking the rules, and now I need to go and handle it."

"But you did all of this because of me," Emily protested. "I feel responsible."

Alyssa gave her a small smile. "I made my own choices. Woods is probably furious with me, but he's only going to be angrier if I bring you along. I have to go and do this, but I wanted to let you know that I won't be available today."

Emily swallowed, not liking the idea of letting Alyssa deal with this alone. "I understand," she said finally.

"Don't look so sad," Alyssa said as she scooted to the end of the booth bench. "This doesn't mean that our investigation is over."

Surprised, Emily tipped her head. "How could it not be? We were told not to do this without his approval. If Woods had any inclination to let us proceed, he certainly won't now."

"Maybe not," she admitted, "but I told you I was after the truth. We're going to find it, but I need you to do me a favor."

"Anything," Emily said immediately.

Alyssa gave her a heavy look, similar to the one she gave to anyone she was on police business and wanted to be taken seriously. "Don't do anything with our investigation without me. If someone did kill Sebastian, then they could just as easily do the same thing to you. I don't want that to happen."

Emily blinked. For some reason, she hadn't thought about that before. "Okay," she stammered. "Good luck."

Alyssa was up and out of the café in a flash, and a moment later her police cruiser flashed by the front windows.

Emily tapped her fingers on the table, feeling impatient and frustrated. She felt absolutely terrible that Alyssa was getting in trouble. Though she hadn't said it aloud, she truly hoped Alyssa wouldn't lose her job over this. It would be all her fault.

Even aside from that possibility, what was she going to do about Sebastian? It seemed likely that she and Alyssa wouldn't have a chance to get back to their quest for quite some time. If Alyssa were allowed to keep her position with the police force, she'd probably have to be very careful to make sure she didn't get in trouble again anytime soon.

"I've waited this long, so a little while longer isn't going to change anything," she told herself as she stared down into her coffee, but as soon as she said it, she knew the words weren't true. She'd already waited so long, and every day that she had to live without Sebastian was a less happy one than it would've been if he were still here. Maybe there was something she could do.

Her mind wandered back to Dillon Dixon. He and his wife had been the last people to see Sebastian alive, and Emily couldn't let go of that fact. Emily had already run into him twice, but she had yet to ask him any questions directly about Sebastian. Feeling resolved, she got the lid for her coffee and left.

It took a bit to find the information on her phone. The screen was tiny compared to looking things up on her laptop, and she hadn't yet gotten into the habit of turning to her phone for every detail she needed. Once she did, she started up the engine.

She and Alyssa may not have been able to see any official records from Phoenix Insurance, which made sense, considering they were asking for a corporation's private paperwork. This was different, Emily reasoned. Nobody would call the police on an old woman who simply wanted to touch base with someone who had been with her husband in the last moments of his life, who could perhaps offer her some comfort in the form of a little bit of clarity.

Rolling to a stop at a traffic light, Emily thought back to that terrible day. She had asked questions, she was sure, but they were panicked questions. Everyone was too busy to tell her much. Her husband was dead in the end regardless, and so those questions had faded from her mind for a time. Until now.

The square gray building was modern and bland, a big block that'd been dropped in amongst the older structure which had some appealing architectural details. Numerous windows covered the sides, but they were all tinted so darkly that they were just as opaque as the rest of the building. A small sign near the door demurely declared it to be Vertex Financial. This was the place that Alyssa had said Dillon worked. All she had to do was ask for him at the front, presumably, and then she would either be turned away or he would invite her in to talk.

As her car door slammed behind her, however, Emily began to question what she was doing. She truly had questions for Dillon, and he was the only one who could really answer them. But what sort of person was she if she showed up at the man's workplace unannounced to ask him about such a sensitive subject? Nobody could question her desire to talk to him, but they could certainly question why she would demand to do so here and now. She would look silly, or maybe even crazy. As she lifted her hand for the door, she dropped it to her side again. Emily stood in front of the door for a moment, wavering, but she turned around and went back to her car.

She would need to talk to Dillon, but she needed to find some other way to do it.

9

There were plenty of things Emily could've done to occupy herself through the rest of the day. Even if she wasn't looking into Sebastian's death, she could just as easily have been working on her blog. She'd managed to get herself behind recently, but she couldn't bring herself to write up a review on anything she'd read lately. Picking up a book she'd recently checked out at the library, she thought perhaps a fresh story would help. Rosemary certainly thought so as she curled up in her lap, but Emily's mind refused to wrap around the new characters and their plights.

All she could think about was Sebastian. What had really happened to him? Had her husband been ripped away from her because it was time, or because someone had some reason to do so? Though she knew there was something fishy about the whole thing, Emily failed to see any reason someone would want to do that. Sebastian had been a loving husband, a caring father, and a responsible worker. She couldn't fault him for a thing, no matter how hard she tried.

Finally, when neither shining up her kitchen sink nor staring at the numerous ingredients in her fridge could bring her out of her funk, Emily gave Rosemary a thorough pet and grabbed her keys.

The sun was working its way down toward the horizon, sending shades of pink and orange up into the sky and streaming down through the cemetery trees. The day had been a warm one, but the coming night was beginning to cool it already. Emily noted the friendly sign on the gate that reminded her the cemetery would be closing at dusk. She wouldn't have a lot of time, but that was all right. She only needed a few minutes to unload her mind and her heart.

In her rush to get out of the house, Emily had forgotten to bring a blanket so that she could sit down next to Sebastian the way she normally did. She shrugged, deciding that scrubbing a few grass stains out of her trousers wouldn't be the end of the world. She certainly didn't feel like standing. Sinking down slowly and ignoring the creak in her knees, she reached out to stroke her fingers over his name.

"I'm sure you're wondering why I'm back again already," she said as she settled onto the ground. "I couldn't wait until our normal visit, Sebastian. My head has been spinning today. There are so many things I want to discuss with you that I don't even know where to start."

A bird swooped overhead, chirping at her on its way. Emily lifted her head to trace its movement into a tree, wondering if it had any cares in the world or if it lived its life day to day.

"I'm sure you know, because I think you know everything, that Alyssa and I are trying to figure out what really happened to you. It's going slowly. I thought I was all right with that. I figured that if I'd already waited this long, then there would be nothing wrong with taking our time and making sure we had everything done correctly before we moved on to the next step.

"It turns out I wasn't really nearly as okay with that as I imagined," she continued with a sigh. "Once we got started, I wanted to skip straight to the end to see how it all came together. I suppose that means I've been watching too many movies lately. Or maybe I just miss you terribly, and I want to be sure that I know the truth."

Her shoulders slumped as she thought about what had happened that day. "Right now, I have to admit that I'm not sure I'll know the truth at all. I suppose I'm j being impatient, but you see, Alyssa has probably gotten in a lot of trouble with her boss. She had to go in to talk to him today, because he'd never given us permission to pursue your case. Now, if you ask me, I shouldn't need any permission at all. You were my husband, and I have every right to know everything. But I do understand that there are procedures in place and whatnot. You can't have everyone out on the street trying to gather up clues and put the story together themselves. It could get chaotic very quickly. Listen to me, rattling on like I always did."

The shadows were deepening. Emily would have to go soon, but she needed to get as much of this off her chest as possible. "At any rate, I haven't heard back from Alyssa since I talked to her this morning. I know she said she wouldn't be available, so I shouldn't expect anything. The girl has a job to do and her own life to live. I can't help but worry, though. What if she and I don't ever get to do this? Alyssa says we will. She's young and confident, and she still sees the world as a place full of possibilities and opportunities. I have to admit I've had my doubts about that, especially lately."

Her phone beeped, pulling her out of her conversation. Hoping that it might be a text message from Alyssa, Emily fished it out of her pocket. It was a voicemail.

"How's that for cell reception?" she joked with Sebastian as she poked at the screen to access her voice messages. "I don't get the call, but I can still get the message."

She gently touched the headstone once again as she waited for the message to play. She hoped that it might be Alyssa, telling her everything was fine and that they could resume their work the next day.

"Mrs. Cherry, this is Chief Inspector Woods," came a stern voice through the line.

Emily's eyes widened. She felt a tightness in her chest that reminded her of how she felt when she was a child and she thought she was in trouble at school. Did Woods want to lecture her about her involvement in this? Had she broken the law? She didn't think so, but he would know better than she. Anita probably knew a good lawyer. She knew everyone.

"It's urgent that I speak with you. I don't like to leave this information in a voicemail, but since I can't seem to get a hold of you I will."

She closed her eyes, waiting for the charges and an order to turn herself in at the police department.

"DC Bradley and I have been discussing the case of your husband's death. Though I don't appreciate that the two of you went ahead behind my back, I've discovered that the original investigation wasn't carried out correctly. There were witness interviews that either didn't happen or that weren't recorded correctly. The entire case was signed off by the former chief inspector, but I can't say that it's anything I ever would've put my stamp of approval on if I were in his place. There's too much missing information, and I plan to look into it."

Relief flooded her system. It sounded as though Alyssa might be in a bit of trouble, but overall things were heading in the right direction. Emily now had not only a fine young detective constable at her back, but the chief inspector as well. That meant things would progress much more quickly, and she and Alyssa would no longer need to tiptoe around so carefully. They would be able to pursue their leads much more easily.

"DC Bradley has gone over all the information that the two of you discussed. She told me about the man who keeps coming to the cemetery. Using city surveillance footage, we were able to gather some more information about him and identify him. His name is Cooper Webb. Given his behavior, we have reason to believe that he could be very dangerous. I advise you to stay away from the cemetery until we have this wrapped up. I'll speak to you again soon." The voicemail ended with a click.

Emily stared at the phone, emotions swirling inside of her. Having the police department's interest and cooperation in the case was incredibly helpful and would help things proceed, but it also meant that she would have to face the truth that she'd been seeking so hard. She felt relief at knowing that Alyssa wasn't going to lose her job, but a shiver of fear rippled through her. Alyssa had warned her that whoever killed Sebastian might turn around and come after her, and Chief Inspector Woods had added his own caveat that this Cooper Webb was dangerous. She needed to get out of here and get home.

A long shadow cast over Sebastian's grave and made Emily look up. Her heart froze as she looked into the face of the mysterious man who'd been coming to the cemetery, who had claimed he was only here to take a walk. He still wore his long gray coat. His cobalt eyes and square jaw were as hard as ever. The only difference between this encounter and the other times she'd seen him was that Cooper Webb was holding a pistol.

10

"Don't move," he growled.

Emily wouldn't dare. She'd been in some harrowing situations over the last few years, but she suddenly realized this was exactly the sort of danger that Nathan was always so worried she would get into. She sent a silent apology through her heart to her son. Maybe he'd been right. She should've lived out the retired life of a little old lady who didn't have anything more exciting in her life than a weekly trip to the library. "I won't."

"Not you." Cooper lifted the barrel of the gun and readjusted the grip in his hand.

Emily's eyes traced the direction of his weapon, and it was then that she realized the two of them weren't alone. Still on the ground, and with electric shivers running up and down her back, she slowly turned to see that Dillon Dixon was standing behind her. He held a gun as well, calmly bracing his forearm against his hip. "I should've figured you'd be here, Cooper."

"Why? Because I actually have a conscience?" The tendons in Cooper's neck twitched as he clenched his jaw.

Dillon laughed, an oddly harsh sound. He had to be at least ten years younger than Cooper, without the wisps of gray showing at his temples. Though he'd always been in a hurry to get away from her every time Emily had seen him, and he'd even been a bit nervous, he looked completely calm right now. One side of his mouth quirked up. "Really? You're going to pretend to stand on high moral ground after everything you did? Do you think playing the hero now is going to erase all of the insurance fraud you committed?"

Emily's eyes bounced back and forth between the two of them as she tried to absorb every detail and figure out what she ought to do about it. They seemed to have more of a problem with each other than with her, though she didn't know why. She didn't even know why they were here, but she wished she wasn't. Getting up and running away wasn't an option. Even at her best, she'd never be able to outrun a bullet. She was stuck.

"Fraud that I committed at your direction." A breeze came through and rippled Cooper's coat. "Not to mention numerous other things that you had me do. I'd hate to actually pause and add up all the violations that you not only approved but blatantly asked for. It's remarkable that Dorris Financial took as long as it did before it went under. It was only your sheer talent for falsifying records that kept you out of jail this long."

This brought out another disturbing chuckle from Dillon. "You thought jumping ship would keep you out of hot water, but I'd be willing to gamble that you didn't do yourself any favors. How far behind are you on the rent right now? Three months, four? It sounds to me like you were much better off when you worked under me. If you had stuck around a little longer and actually been loyal, you might be doing as well as I am now."

Emily clutched her fingers in the grass, wishing she had some sort of defense at her disposal. So, Dillon had worked for Dorris Financial. That must have been how Sebastian had come to know him. Cooper worked there as well, that much was clear. But what was their connection with her? The massive amounts of fear and adrenaline that mixed in her brain weren't helping her think. They only made her want to run.

Cooper wasn't fazed by the way Dillon tried to mock him. "Those big bonuses you offered me back in those days only lasted so long, it's true. But every scheme has its expiration date. You can't rip people off forever and expect to get away with it. It's a hard lesson to learn, and I'm ashamed to say that I had to learn it for myself, but I'm even more ashamed that you haven't."

Dillon shrugged, causing him to gesture slightly with his gun. "I don't know what made you get so high and mighty. It was never anything personal. It's not like we were knocking down old ladies on the street and stealing their purses. It was insurance money, stuff that comes from big corporations that hardly affects their bottom line at all. Don't forget that you agreed with me for a long time."

"Sure, until I realized that none of it was as simple as you said it would be," Cooper replied. "As a matter of fact, there were a lot of things that didn't turn out the way you said. You thought this little scheme of yours could go on forever, but then Sebastian caught onto us."

Emily's stomach clung to her spine. Her heart rattled in her chest like a rock in a tin can, and she hardly knew what to think. She'd been looking so hard for the clues that would lead her to the truth of her husband's death, and now it seemed that they'd come right to her. It was overwhelming.

"I came to you," Cooper said, his brows lowering and his voice breaking slightly. "I came to you because I knew it was over. Sebastian was a smart man, and he was good at his job. He knew that all those claims had to be fraudulent, because even fleet vehicles don't get wrecked that often. He might not have guessed the entirety of the truth, that you had someone under your thumb that would do the repair work for next to nothing while we pocketed the rest, but he knew it wasn't right."

"He liked to stick his nose where it didn't belong. His first mistake was in trying to tell you about it instead of going straight to his boss or to the police. He obviously wasn't as smart as you think he was." Dillon dared to roll his eyes.

"He was trying to be kind, something that you obviously don't understand. Sebastian told me what he knew because he thought I was being taken advantage of. He didn't want me to go down with the rest of the ship if I was being used as a pawn. I was, but not in the way he imagined. There are many ways of being smart, Dillon, and more respectable ways than yours."

She pressed her hand down into the grass and dirt underneath her, trying to steady herself and wishing Sebastian was here. She had to do something about all of this, but what? She wondered what Alyssa would do, but she was a trained police officer. All Emily could do for now was to cling to what scraps they were giving her and hoping she could piece them all together when this was over with. Provided, of course, that she got out alive.

"I was the one who made a mistake in coming to you," Cooper told the other man. "I let my fear rule my head, and that's a decision I've regretted ever since."

"I told you I would take care of it, and I did," Dillon retorted easily.

"Yes, but I never thought you meant something like taking him out to sea and killing him." Cooper's mouth tightened.

Her head grew dizzy as she looked back and forth, wondering if the two of them even knew if she was still there. Sebastian. Her dear Sebastian. It had been no accident. She had the truth she wanted, and it hurt far more than she ever could've imagined. She wasn't sure if the men even knew she was there anymore.

Dillon's gun swiveled down to point straight at her, answering her question without it having to be asked. "So, what do you want, Cooper? You want me to go to jail? Because let me remind you that you'll be in the very next cell if the old lady rats on us. She's already been on our tail. She's been snooping around my boat, and earlier today she showed up at my office. She looks innocent, but she knows. I wouldn't doubt that she's been trying to find information on you, too. Isn't that right, Emily?"

Her stomach dropped straight through the earth when Dillon's dark eyes pivoted down to meet hers. Emily gaped at him. Fear gripped her, but then she thought of Sebastian. She had loved her husband more than life itself, and this man had taken him away. Her fear subsided as anger took over. "How dare you? You did all of this purely for profit, for greed, without thinking about what it would do to anyone else. And then when your secret is about to come out, you resort to murder? Do you really think it was worth it? Is your fancy boat worth the price you'll have to pay in the long run? Someone ought to teach you a lesson!"

"You see?" Dillon said, addressing Cooper once again. "She's a liability just like her husband was. It's a moment of your life compared to the entirety of it in jail.

Cooper nodded and pointed his gun straight at her.

Emily closed her eyes. She'd made her peace with God a long time ago. Now she could only think of everyone she would be leaving behind, because there was no way for her to get out of this. She thought of sweet Rosemary, of Anita. Of her three beautiful children that had grown into successful adults, and their spouses that had become part of the family. Of Alyssa, who had tried so hard to help her and now would never know the truth that Emily had discovered.

The gun fired. Emily waited for the pain, but it didn't come. Something flapped past her, the sunlight and shadow flickering in her vision. Emily opened her eyes. Dillon lay writhing on the ground, clutching his upper arm where blood leaked out from between his fingers. Cooper stood over him, pulling Dillon's gun from his limp hand. His face was hard as he quickly and expertly emptied the guns of their bullets, letting the clips fall to the ground.

Then he turned and reached out a hand to Emily. "Are you all right?"

She wasn't even sure she could stand up. Her ears were ringing, though whether it was from the gunfire or the new information she wasn't sure. She stumbled to her feet, leaning heavily on his arm. A high-pitched noise rose and fell in her ears. "I'm not sure."

Cooper's sapphire eyes met hers. "I've felt guilty all these years for what Dillon did to your husband. I wasn't about to let him do the same to you."

11

A warm blanket fell around her shoulders and a hot drink was pressed into her hands. Emily looked up to see Alyssa's concerned face. Emergency lights flickered across her face from the numerous vehicles that were now parked around the cemetery. "Are you sure you're all right?"

Emily felt so strange that she didn't know how to describe it. She was all right in terms of being physically whole. Beyond her knees being a little sore from too much time on the ground, and a little bit of exhaustion, she was going to be just fine. Dillon Dixon, who could be heard moaning and cursing as he was loaded into one of the waiting ambulances, wasn't faring quite as well. Not that Emily felt sorry for him in the least.

"I am," she finally said. "It's going to take me some time to process this, and I imagine I'm going to feel a bit strange until then. I doubted myself when I questioned whether Sebastian's death was truly an accident, but now I know the truth in its entirety."

Alyssa put her arm around Emily's shoulders. "How are you feeling about that?"

Her head was still spinning, but it had at least slowed down a bit. "It's uncomfortable, but I'm glad to know that his killer will get the justice he deserves. Overall, it's a good thing. Could I ask you a favor?"

"Of course."

"I'd like to have you with me when I tell my children. They're going to want to know a lot of details, and they deserve to know them, but I just don't know that I can do it on my own. It's going to break their hearts, in a way, as it has mine. I know it will bring them some peace at the same time."

"Anything you need, Emily. Anything you need at all," Alyssa whispered quietly.

"Speaking of, perhaps you could tell me how the police and ambulances turned up so quickly. I think I heard the sirens coming right after Cooper shot Dillon, but that doesn't make sense. I hadn't told anyone but Rosemary that I was coming to the cemetery, and of course none of us had a clue that either of those men would show up here."

"Do you remember Hugo Williams, the groundskeeper we spoke to?" Alyssa pointed through the chaos of the scene to where another officer was interviewing him. Judging by the grin on the old man's face, Hugo was still telling his jokes.

"Hard to forget someone like him," Emily admitted.

Alyssa nodded. "And he hadn't forgotten the promise that he made to us. He saw the mysterious man that we'd described to him, and he called me right away. Chief Inspector Woods and I had just figured out who he was not long before that."

"Yes, I'd received his message when it was a bit too late. What made you think Cooper was dangerous?" Emily searched through the pulsing lights and the numerous cars and people to find the no-longer-mysterious man, who was sitting with his hands cuffed behind his back. Both he and the officers around him were perfectly calm as he was questioned.

"We didn't have a lot to go on," Alyssa admitted. "Once we had his identity, it was easy enough to find out that he'd worked for Dorris Financial. Knowing that, plus the fact that he'd come to the cemetery so often, made us believe that he very well might be after you."

Emily shook her head and looked down into the cup that was still in her hands. It looked to be weak coffee. She took a sip. It was terrible. "He was grieving, t as I was. He felt responsible for Sebastian's death, and he couldn't do anything about it without turning himself in."

"Yes. I caught a little bit of his questioning. It seems that he's felt somewhat responsible for you ever since Sebastian's death, and he's kept an eye on Dillon Dixon as well. He put a few pieces together and figured you were trying to uncover the truth. He knew Dillon would come after you, and so he came here tonight." Alyssa pulled a deep breath in through her nose and let it out slowly. "This has been one of the strangest cases I've ever worked on."

"Speaking of, are you going to be able to work on more of them in the future?" Emily reached over and tapped her badge. "I see you're still wearing that, so I assume Chief Inspector Woods didn't fire you."

She smiled, and it looked to be one of relief. "No, but he certainly wasn't pleased. The fact that the original investigation wasn't conducted properly really saved my hide. It made him want to know more, like us, and we spent all afternoon poring over it. The department has some pretty good resources at its fingertips, so we were able to make quick progress when it came to Cooper. He wasn't exactly our man, but he still led us all to the right one."

Emily looked over at him again. "Do you think I could have a moment to talk to him before you take him away?"

Alyssa looked doubtful, but she nodded. "If you'd like."

She escorted Emily over to the arrestee and murmured to a few of the other officers. They stepped back, and Cooper looked at her sadly.

Emily clasped her hands in front of her. They were chilly in the night air, even though she still wore the blanket like a cape. "Cooper, I'd like to thank you."

His head shot back in surprise. "How can you possibly thank me after what I've done?"

It was a good question, and she understood why he asked it. But Emily felt as though she had a whole new perspective on life after this. Perhaps it was because she thought she was going to die, or maybe it was because she'd discovered a bigger truth that was far more important than herself. Either way, she knew this was the right thing. "First of all, you saved my life."

Cooper opened his mouth to protests, but then he closed it and nodded. "I did, and I'd do it again. I've been trying to keep an eye on Dillon, worried about what else he might do, and so I was lucky enough to be in the right place at the right time. I only wish I could've done the same for Sebastian."

Emily was so tired. She couldn't remember ever being this fatigued, not even when her children were babies and would keep her up half the night. She leaned against a squad car and pulled the blanket closer around her. "We can't change the past. No matter how much we regret what we've done, we don't get a chance to do things over. You didn't know that Dillon was going to kill Sebastian."

Cooper looked away, shame covering his face. "No, but I should've known. I knew what a hard man he was, and that he would go to great lengths to get what he wanted. Not that it's an excuse, but I thought everything he and I were doing together at Dorris Financial was all about money and nothing more. I hope you can believe that I would've made completely different decisions if I'd realized what Dillon was capable of."

"I know." She'd heard his entire conversation with Dillon, and she'd heard the passion and sorrow in his voice as he spoke his side. "I also know that Sebastian must have seen something very good in you if he came to you about the insurance fraud. That means something to me. He wanted to give you a chance to make it right."

"Yes, he did." Cooper swallowed, remembering. His brows scrunched together and then relaxed as several expressions rippled across his face. Emily could imagine the emotional turmoil he was going through right now. "I only wish there was something I could do to make it all up to you."

Emily shook her head. There was nothing Cooper could do to bring Sebastian back or to take away the heartache she'd experienced at not having him in in her life. It was a toll that was impossible to pay back. Even so, Emily had an idea forming in her brain. It was too new for the moment, and she needed some time to work with it when she had a little more capacity to think. "There might be something you can do for me, Cooper, but I'll have to let you know."

"You take care of yourself, Emily." His voice was quiet, sincere.

"Thank you. I will. You do the same."

Emily stepped back over to Alyssa, and the plans to clear out the cemetery began to commence. Hugo Williams looked disappointed by this, thrilled to have so many people to talk to. Cooper was put in the back of a cruiser and taken to the station. The ambulance carrying Dillon was already long gone. The remainder of the emergency crews put their equipment away, turned off their lights, and cleared out. Alyssa insisted on driving Emily home and having her little sedan driven by one of the other officers.

"Are you really all right?" Alyssa asked when they were inside the warm interior of her car once again. "I know this has been hard. If you need me to stay with you for a while when we get back to your place, I can do that."

Emily looked back at Sebastian's grave, barely visible. She should be terrified and shaken. She should be angry and upset, and she ought to be railing at a universe that would allow such a terrible thing to happen. But a sense of peace fell over her, relaxing her shoulders and driving all the spiraling thoughts out of her mind. She was more relaxed, she realized, than she'd been in a long time. "No, that's all right. I think I just want to go to sleep."

12

The headphones clamped down on her ears. There were so many knobs and buttons that Emily couldn't imagine what they all even did. Her heartbeat was high and thready with nerves, but Toby was grinning at her. She must be doing all right.

"It's an incredible story, Emily." Toby, for once not wearing a grocery store apron or helping her find food, was wearing a band t-shirt while seated comfortably on a stool in his garage. His hair was a bright electric blue this time. "I think it's made you a bit of a local celebrity."

"Oh, I don't know about that." She blushed, even though nobody could see her but Toby. Emily hadn't been sure about coming on his podcast, and in fact she didn't think she belonged on it at all. He usually talked about music and local bands. When she'd tried to listen in to be supportive of him, she usually got lost.

But Toby had insisted that everyone would want to hear from her, as he was now. "It's true! You've been in the paper and on the news. People are talking about you all over social media. If anyone in Little Oakley hasn't heard about you, then they must be living under a rock. Honestly, I can understand why. Most of us don't have the courage to do what you've done."

"I'm not really that special," Emily countered. "I just knew that something wasn't quite right, and I wanted to explore it. I was fortunate enough to have a lot of the right people around me. I never would've gotten anywhere without the help of the Little Oakley Police Department, specifically DC Alyssa Bradley and Chief Inspector Woods, as well as my best friend and my children. I should even thank my cat, I suppose. Rosemary has been there for me ever since my husband died, and she makes everything more bearable." She smiled, knowing that Alyssa would be getting a promotion out of this whole ordeal. It was the least she deserved.

Toby nodded. "Absolutely. I think we can all relate to that. So, what's next for you?"

This was something she'd thought long and hard about. The idea had occurred to her several times, though she'd never believed that she was truly ready. Now was the time, because she didn't see any point in waiting any longer. "I'm going to write a book." The words felt good, and she knew she'd made the right decision in making the announcement here.

"That's awesome!" Toby enthused. "Will it be a book about your experience with this case, I assume?"

"Yes," she said with a happy sigh. "I think there's a lot of information to cover, more than I can recite during an interview. Sebastian deserves to have his story out there. I've wanted to write a book for a long time, and now I think I finally have the perfect thing to write about."

"There's nobody more qualified than you, that's for sure. It looks like our time is about up. Is there anything else that you want people to know before you go?" Toby raised an eyebrow.

Emily froze for a second, unsure of what to say, but then she remembered what one of her primary missions in life had been recently. "Yes. I'd like to remind people to stop by Best Friends Furever. Even if you aren't interested in adopting a dog or cat right now, they could use your help with donations or your time. Lily Austin would be happy to speak with you."

"Okay, folks. There you have it. You be sure to check in with Best Friends Furever, and I'll be sure to check in again with our own Emily Cherry on her upcoming book. Thanks again for stopping by, Emily."

"Thank you."

Toby touched a few buttons. A hard guitar riff sounded and then faded out, and he took off his headphones. "That was great, Emily. I can't thank you enough."

"It was my pleasure. I only hope that I didn't chase your usual listeners away." She rose from the chair he'd provided for her, an old desk chair that was much more comfortable than the stool he was sitting on.

"Not at all. I think they'll love it. I'll walk you out." He hit a button on the wall, opening the garage door and letting the sun shine in.

"I'm proud of you, Toby," she said as she walked out to her car. "I like seeing you do what you love."

"I guess that makes two of us. You make sure you let me know how the book is going. I'll see you in the store soon, I'm sure."

"Yes, I'm sure you will!" Emily smiled as she drove across town and parked at Alexandria's Books. She would need to get home and spend some time writing her own book, but she also knew what an inspiration it was to read those by others.

She stepped inside to the familiar scent of books and ink. Two customers were crowded at the counter with Stewart, but they turned around as soon as she walked in.

"Emily!" Eliana Palmer turned around and immediately enfolded Emily in her long arms. "I heard! I'm so excited for you! I'm always happy to have more author friends!"

"Now, don't give me too much credit. You're the real author." Eliana had written a few fantasy books that were quite popular.

"I'm not different from you," Eliana countered. "Speaking of authors, though, I'd like to introduce you to Brayden Bell." She gestured at the other man standing there with her.

Brayden Bell had friendly eyes and shaggy brown hair. He eagerly stepped forward to shake her hand. "I understand that it's all thanks to you that I'm no longer in prison. I'd been wanting to thank you for that, but I've been a little bit busy getting my life straightened out."

"I can imagine!" Brayden had been framed by his ex-girlfriend for a crime he hadn't committed, and Emily had been instrumental in discovering the truth. "It's very nice to meet you."

"And you, too. You be sure to let us know when your book is out. We'll be the first to buy it," Brayden promised as Eliana nodded her agreement.

"And I'll be the first store to stock it," Stewart promised. "I've already been thinking about how your window display will look. We can do some author signing events. I'll probably need to order some more chairs..."

"You're getting too far ahead of yourself!" Emily laughed. "I haven't even written the first word yet. I'm still in the planning stages, and even then, I haven't gotten very far. There's a lot of work to be done, but I'll be sure to give you plenty of time to order chairs."

"Sounds good! You should get some other promotional materials, too, like maybe some bookmarks or magnets," he suggested.

"Stewart!" Emily was laughing hard now. The very idea was making her giddy, and she loved that she had so much support. "I'll contact you when the time is right."

When she'd made her purchase and bid goodbye, Emily headed down the street and sat down breathlessly across from Anita at The Daydream Café.

"Well, I'm surprised that the woman of the hour has any time for me at all," Anita said with a catty smile. "You're positively famous, dear. I'm going to attach myself solidly to you so that I can soak up some of that star power."

"All right, but you only have a short amount of time to do it in," Emily teased back. "I've got to get over to see Cooper at our appointed time. The warden is kind enough to give me a generous visiting time, but I wouldn't want to irritate him."

Anita smiled. "I think it's wonderful that he's agreed to help you this way, and I also think it's wonderful what you're doing for him. It gives him a chance to fully tell his side of the story, which he might not get to do otherwise."

"I think he's helping me out far more than I'm helping him, but I'm glad that we're able to work together." This was the thought that had occurred to her when he'd expressed his wish to make it all up to her. She hadn't been completely certain in the moment, especially since she'd been so deluged with the facts of her husband's death. The more she'd considered it, however, the more sense it made. Cooper had been more than happy to oblige.

"Do we know yet how long he'll be staying behind bars?" Anita asked quietly.

"There are still some proceedings to go through. He has quite a few charges of insurance fraud against him, but the fact that he's testifying against Dillon Dixon is going to help him negotiate. He said he's actually relieved that this has all come to a head, even if it means he's in prison for the moment. He doesn't have to keep his secret anymore, and it's a lot easier on him."

"And what about you?" Anita gave her a pointed look. "Is it easier on you? Knowing what really happened?"

"Yes," Emily said with confidence. "I know it doesn't seem like it should be, but I feel like this means I can finally put it all behind me. Nathan, Phoebe, and Mavis are all on board with me writing the book, too. It'll be therapeutic to put it all out there and then move on with our lives. Not that I'll really ever have moved on from Sebastian, of course, but I won't be wondering any more. That takes up a lot more energy than one would think."

"I'm sure. And your blog? Are you giving it up now that you have a book to write?"

It was a question that everyone had been asking, and Emily had always been certain of the answer. "Absolutely not. I've finally found the perfect formula for it, one that works both for me and for my readers. I wouldn't dare give up my posts that help out the shelter, either. I'll be spending a lot of time writing, but I'm quite happy about that."

The two of them sat there for a while together, chatting about the weather and where they might go shopping that weekend. They had been through a lot together, but they were still a couple of girlfriends, no matter how much time passed.

After a bit, though, Anita needed to get going. Emily sat for a moment, taking in the atmosphere of the café around her. Then she got out her laptop and opened her word processor. The blank page was a bit intimidating, but her blogging experience had taught her that sometimes the best thing to do was simply to write. It didn't have to be perfect. It didn't even have to be close. She only needed to get started.

The mysteries we read in a book or watch on a screen are fun and exciting. We're happy to point out the killer and crow that we knew who it was all along. But have you ever stopped to think what it's like when you really do know all along?

I did, in a way. I just didn't believe or trust in myself enough to realize it at first.

THANK YOU FOR CHOOSING A PUREREAD BOOK!

We hope you enjoyed the story, and as a way to thank you for choosing PureRead we'd like to send you this free Special Edition Cozy, and other fun reader rewards...

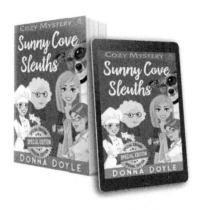

Click Here to download your free Cozy Mystery
PureRead.com/cozy

Thanks again for reading.

See you soon!

OTHER BOOKS IN THIS SERIES

If you loved this story and want to follow Emily's antics in other fun easy read mysteries continue **dive straight into other books in this series...**

Read them all...

A Troubling Case Of Murder On The Menu

A Crafty Case Of Murder At The Fair

A Hairy Case of Murder At The Animal Sanctuary

A Clean & Tidy Case of Murder - A Truly Messy Mystery

A Cranky Case of Murder at the Autostore

A Colorful Case of Stolen Art at the Gallery

A Frightful Case of Murder in the Fashion Store

A Beastly Case of Murder at the Bookstore

A Murky Case of Murder at the Movies

OUR GIFT TO YOU

AS A WAY TO SAY THANK YOU WE WOULD
LOVE TO SEND YOU THIS SPECIAL EDITION
COZY MYSTERY FREE OF CHARGE.

Our Reader List is 100% FREE

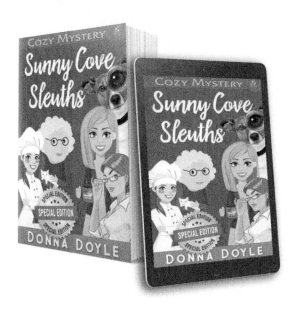

Click Here to download your free Cozy Mystery
PureRead.com/cozy

At PureRead we publish books you can trust. Great tales without smut or swearing, but with all of the mystery and romance you expect from a great story.

Be the first to know when we release new books, take part in our fun competitions, and get surprise free books in your inbox by signing up to our Reader list.

As a thank you you'll receive this exclusive Special Edition Cozy available only to our subscribers...

Click Here to download your free Cozy Mystery
PureRead.com/cozy

Thanks again for reading.
See you soon!

Printed in Great Britain
by Amazon

41787284R10061